KU-067-255

WITHDRAWN FROM STOCK

Don't dawdle DOROTHY!

Margrit Cruickshank
Illustrated by Amanda Harvey

FRANCES LINCOLN

Dorothy and her mother went shopping.
They shopped all morning.

Dorothy was tired . . .

and it was a very long way home.
"Don't dawdle, Dorothy!" said her mother.

Dorothy sighed, and shut her eyes.
When she opened them, in front
of her was ...

a wicked witch with long straggly hair and a pointy black hat.

"Don't dawdle, Dorothy!" said the witch.

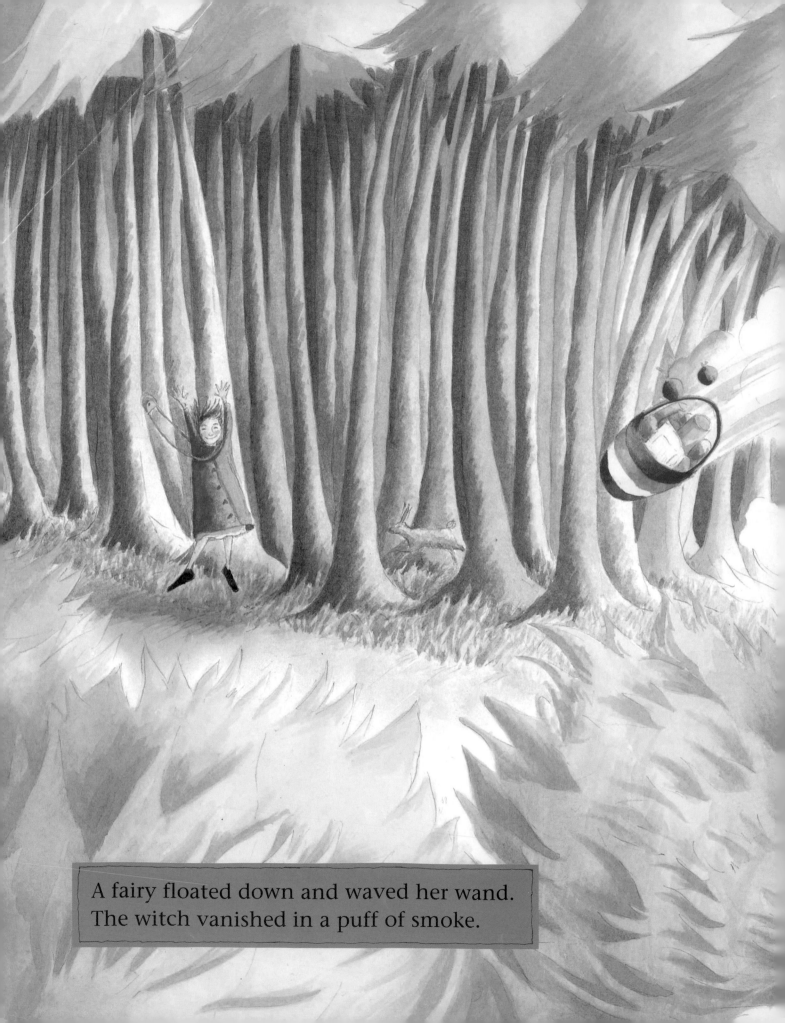

A fairy floated down and waved her wand.
The witch vanished in a puff of smoke.

Pff!

Dorothy dawdled up the hill behind
a Snow Queen with icicles for fingernails
and eyes as deep and cold as icebergs.

"Don't dawdle, Dorothy!"
said the Snow Queen.

The sun came out and the Snow Queen melted into a shiny wet puddle.

Splish!

Dorothy dawdled up the hill behind
an ogre who was as tall as a block of flats
and as broad as a barn.

"Don't dawdle, Dorothy!" said the ogre.

A mouse darted out of the sunflower field and scared the ogre away.

Squeak!

Dorothy dawdled up the hill behind a grumpy old bear.

CITY OF LIMERICK
PUBLIC LIBRARY

"Don't dawdle, Dorothy!"
said the bear.

A tiger crouching in the bushes grinned,
wriggled its lean, mean hindquarters
and pounced on the grumpy old bear.

Dorothy dawdled up the hill behind an alien from outer space, with a body like an elephant's and eyes on stalks at the top of its head.

"Don't dawdle, Dorothy!" said the alien.

A space ship whizzed over the treetops and sucked the alien up, just like a vacuum cleaner!

Slurp!

Dorothy couldn't go one more step.
She sighed, and shut her eyes.
When she opened them . . .

her mother turned and smiled at her.
"Nearly there, Dorothy," she said . . .

46486

"I'll give you a piggy-back home."
And she did.

CITY OF LIMERICK
PUBLIC LIBRARY